VALERIE THOMAS AND KORKY PAUL

Winnie and Wilbur
TRICKS AND TREATS

Winnie and Wilbur: WINNIE THE WITCH

Winnie and Wilbur: THE MIDNIGHT DRAGON

Winnie and Wilbur: THE HAUNTED HOUSE

Winnie AND Wilbur
WINNIE THE WITCH

Winnie the Witch lived in a
black house in the forest.
The house was black on the
outside and black on the inside.
The carpets were black.
The chairs were black.
The bed was black and it had
black sheets and black blankets.
Even the bath was black.

Winnie lived in her black house with her cat, Wilbur.
He was black too. And that is how the trouble began.

When Wilbur sat on a chair with
his eyes open, Winnie could see him.
She could see his eyes, anyway.

But when Wilbur closed his eyes and went to sleep, Winnie couldn't see him at all. So she sat on him.

When Wilbur sat on the carpet with his eyes open, Winnie could see him. She could see his eyes, anyway.

But when Wilbur closed his
eyes and went to sleep,
Winnie couldn't see him at all.
So she tripped over him.

One day, after a nasty fall, Winnie
decided something had to be done.
She picked up her magic wand,
waved it once and **Abracadabra!**
Wilbur was a black cat no longer.
He was bright green!

'Abracadabra!'

Now, when Wilbur slept on a chair, Winnie could see him.

When Wilbur slept on the floor, Winnie could see him.

And she could see him
when he slept on the bed.
But, Wilbur was not allowed
to sleep on the bed . . .

. . . so Winnie put
him outside.
Outside in
the grass.

Winnie came hurrying outside,
tripped over Wilbur,
turned three somersaults,
and fell into a rose bush.

When Wilbur sat outside in the grass,
Winnie couldn't see him, even when
his eyes were wide open.

This time, Winnie was furious.
She picked up her magic wand,
waved it five times and . . .

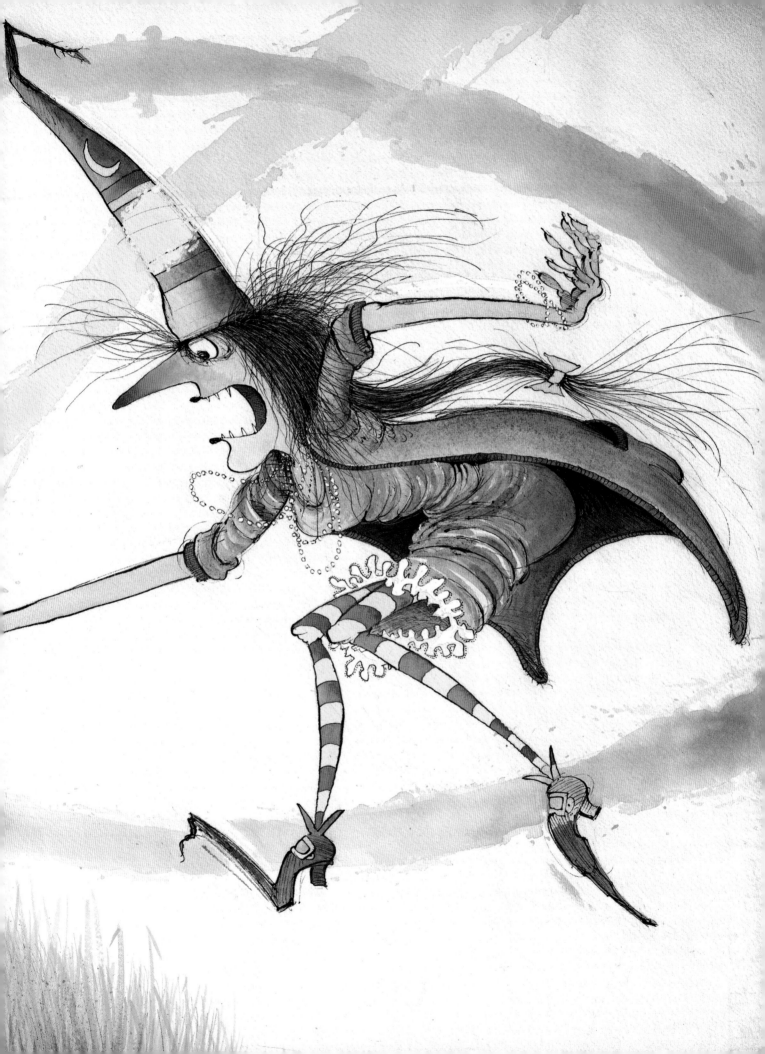

. . . Abracadabra! Wilbur had a red head,
a yellow body, a pink tail, blue whiskers,
and four purple legs.
But his eyes were still green.

Now, Winnie could see Wilbur when
he sat on a chair, when he lay on the
carpet, when he crawled into the grass.

And even when
he climbed
to the top
of the
tallest
tree.

Wilbur climbed to the top of the tallest tree to hide.
He looked ridiculous and he knew it.
Even the birds laughed at him.

Wilbur was miserable.
He stayed at the top
of the tree all day
and all night.

Next morning Wilbur
was still up the tree.
Winnie was worried.
She loved Wilbur
and hated him to
be miserable.

Then Winnie had an idea.
She waved her magic wand
and **Abracadabra!**
Wilbur was a black cat once more.
He came down from the tree, purring.

Then Winnie waved her wand again, and again, and again.

'Abracadabra!'

Now instead of a black house,
she had a yellow house with a
red roof and a red door.
The chairs were white with red
and white cushions. The carpet
was green with pink roses.

The bed was blue, with pink and
white sheets and pink blankets.
The bath was a gleaming white.

And now, Winnie can see Wilbur
no matter where he sits.

Winnie and Wilbur
THE MIDNIGHT DRAGON

'Time for bed,' said Winnie the Witch,
as the clock struck twelve.
Witches always go to bed at midnight.
Winnie turned off the lights and went upstairs.

She brushed her teeth, washed her face,
put on her nightie and climbed into bed.
In two minutes she was snoring.

Wilbur, her big black cat, was already asleep.
He was curled up in his basket, dreaming.

Two minutes later, Wilbur woke up.
He could hear a funny noise in the garden.

He crept to the cat flap and peeped out.
There was something on the door mat.
Something with big green eyes.

'Meeoww!' cried Wilbur
and he jumped back.
A long nose poked
through the cat flap.

Then there was a puff of smoke.
The cat flap wobbled and shook.

A spiky body, then a long tail, followed the nose.
There was a baby dragon in Winnie's house!
'Meeoww!' cried Wilbur. He turned three
backward somersaults and ran into the hall.

The baby dragon thought this was fun.
He ran after Wilbur.
Swish, swish went his tail.
Winnie's grandfather clock wobbled and shook.

DING!   DONG!   BOING!

'Meeoww!' cried Wilbur and he raced upstairs.
The baby dragon ran after him.
Swish, swish went his tail.
Winnie's suit of armour wobbled
and shook and rolled down the stairs.

CRASH!   BANG!   CLANG!

'Meeoww!' cried Wilbur outside Winnie's door.
Winnie woke up and jumped out of bed.
'Whatever's that?' she said.

Then she saw a puff of smoke coming
from behind her broomstick.
'Oh no!' said Winnie. 'My broomstick is on fire!'

Winnie grabbed her broomstick.
'Goodness gracious me!' said Winnie.
'It's a baby dragon! He could burn my house down.
We'll have to find his mother, Wilbur.'

'Where's your mother, little dragon?'
Winnie asked.
'Boo hoo hoo,' cried the baby dragon.

A cloud of smoke came out of his nose.
Puff, puff.

Then Winnie had an idea.
She waved her magic wand three times, and shouted,

'Abracadabra!'

'Puff!' went the dragon,
and out of his nose came . . .

a cloud of butterflies.
'Puff, puff, puff,' went the baby dragon,
who was very surprised.

SMASH!
went Winnie's best bowl.

SPLASH!
went the vase of flowers.

There were butterflies everywhere.
Wilbur loved chasing butterflies.
The baby dragon loved chasing anything!

CRASH!
went the table.

'That wasn't such a good idea,' said Winnie.
She waved her magic wand again, and shouted,

'Abracadabra!'

Out of the dragon's nose came . . .
Nothing.

'Good,' said Winnie. 'Now let's get some sleep.'
But the baby dragon didn't want to sleep.
He wanted to play.

'Bother!' said Winnie.
'We'd better find your mother right now!'

She got a torch and went out onto the roof.
'Yoo hoo,' she called.

It was quiet and dark on the roof.
'Yoo hoo,' Winnie called again,
and waved her torch.

Suddenly there was a flash of fire,
and the sound of great wings.
The baby dragon jumped up and down.
'Mamamamama,' he called.
'Yoo hoo hoo!' called Winnie.

But the baby dragon's mother didn't see them.
Then Winnie had a wonderful idea.

She grabbed her wand,
waved it six times, shouted,

'Abracadabra!'

and there, above her house,
was an enormous moon.

The mother dragon came flying back.
She swooped down and scooped up her baby.

'Wait a minute!' called Winnie.
She waved her magic wand, and shouted,

'Abracadabra!'

'Puff!' went the baby dragon and smoke
came out of his nose again.

The two dragons flew high into the sky and disappeared.

Winnie waved her wand, shouted,

'Abracadabra!'

and the enormous moon went out.
'Now let's go back to bed, Wilbur,' she said.

Winnie climbed into bed and shut her eyes.
In half a minute she was snoring.
Wilbur was already asleep in his basket.

Just then, the sun rose. The night was over.
But Winnie the Witch and Wilbur were fast asleep.

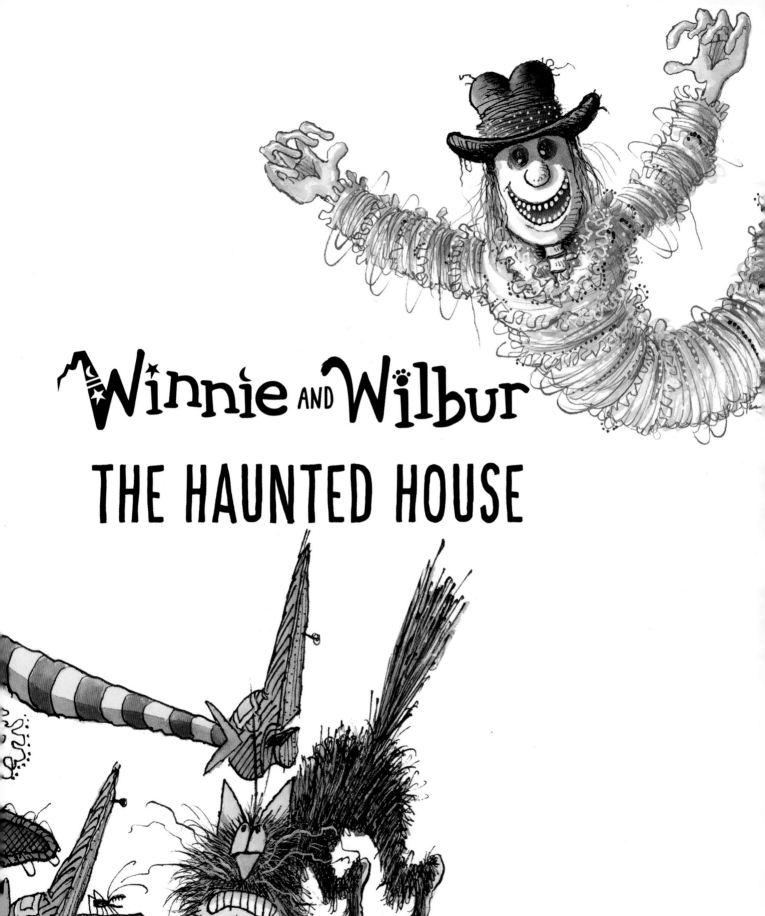

Winnie and Wilbur

THE HAUNTED HOUSE

It was a lovely, warm,
sunny afternoon.
Winnie the Witch thought
she'd have a sleep.

She sat down in her big armchair,
shut her eyes, and in two minutes
she was snoring.

Wilbur, Winnie's big black cat,
thought he'd have a sleep, too.

He curled up on a cushion,
shut his eyes, and in three minutes . . .

a bumblebee flew in
through the window.

Buzzzzz!

Wilbur liked to chase bumblebees.
He jumped up at the bumblebee,

and missed.

He jumped up again . . . . higher . . .

missed the bumblebee . . .

and landed . . .

in the big vase of flowers
on Winnie's table.

CRASH! SMASH! SPLASH!

Winnie woke up.
'Oh no! My best vase!' she said.
'Did you do that, Wilbur?'
But she couldn't see
Wilbur anywhere.

'Where are my glasses?'
asked Winnie.
'Who took them?'

She bent down to look for them.

Wilbur shot out from
under Winnie's chair.
Where could he hide?

Behind the curtains.

SWISH! CRASH!
Down came the curtains, on top of Winnie.

'Blithering broomsticks!'
she shouted.
Winnie crawled out from
under the curtains.
'Who did that? Was it a ghost?
Is my house haunted?'

Wilbur raced up the stairs.
Where could he hide?

Then he saw the perfect place.
Winnie would never look up there.

Wilbur jumped onto the banister
and then sprang onto the chandelier.

The chandelier swung
from side to side.

Wilbur hung on tightly.

Perhaps the chandelier
wasn't a good idea.

Wilbur jumped back onto
the banister just in time.

CRASH!

It definitely wasn't a good idea.

Winnie rushed into the hall.
'My beautiful chandelier!'
she cried. 'My house *is* haunted.
There must be a spell to fix a
haunted house.'

Winnie picked up her Big
Book of Spells and quickly
turned over the pages.
Yes, there it was: a spell for
fixing a haunted house.
Wasn't it?
It was hard to read it
without her glasses.

She shut her eyes,
stamped her foot three times,
waved her magic wand,
and shouted,

'Abracadabra!'

There was a
great gust of wind
and everything went dark.
Owls and bats flew overhead.
Skeletons rattled on the staircases.
Spiders' webs hung from the ceilings,
thick with hairy spiders. Ghosts slithered
through the walls. '**Woo, wooo**,' they cried.
Winnie's house *really* was a haunted house.

Whoosh!

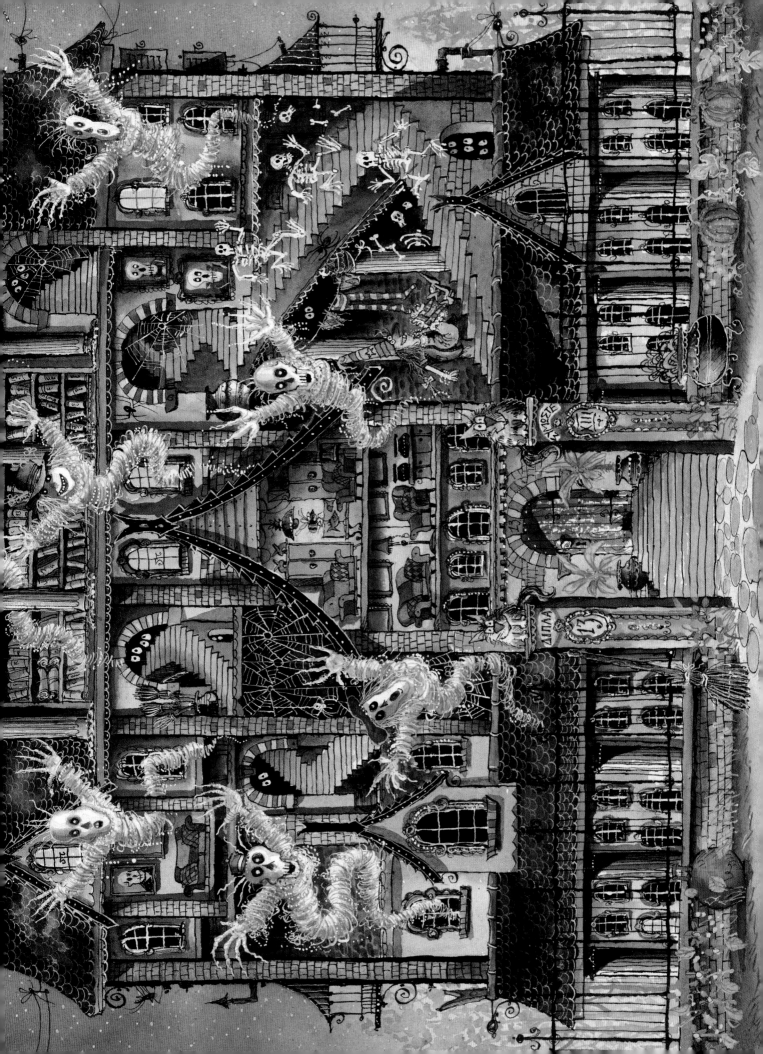

'**Boo!**'

shouted a ghost.
Winnie was very surprised.

She jumped back,
into a sticky spider's web.

A big hairy spider tickled her nose.

'Urk! Yuck! A-a-a-chooo!'

Wilbur came running down the stairs.
'Meeow, meeeow,' he cried.

'Don't be frightened, Wilbur,'
Winnie said. 'I must have made
a mistake with my spell.'

She looked in the Big Book of Spells again,
and a swooping owl knocked her glasses onto her nose.
'So that's where they were,' she said.
Winnie looked carefully at the spell.

Winnie looked at the next spell.
It said:

To FIX ⭐ a Haunted House DO the haunting spell backwards.

'That should work,'
Winnie said.

She opened her eyes wide,
waved her foot high in the air three times,
waved her wand backwards,
and shouted,

'Arbadacarba!'

WHOOSH!

All was quiet. Winnie's haunted house was Winnie's house again. But it was a very messy house.

There were bits of vase, heaps of curtains, and chunks of chandelier everywhere.

'Never mind,' Winnie said. 'I'll soon clean it up.'
She waved her magic wand, shouted,

'Abracadabra!'

. . . and the vase, the curtains, and the
chandelier were as good as new.
'That's a very useful spell,' Winnie said.

Then Winnie sat down in an armchair.
She thought she'd finish her sleep.
Wilbur climbed onto her lap.
He really needed a sleep.

'We've had an exciting day, haven't we, Wilbur,'
Winnie said. 'I don't suppose I'll ever know
what *was* haunting my house.'

I hope not, Wilbur thought.
'Purr, purr, purr,' he said.

OXFORD
UNIVERSITY PRESS

Great Clarendon Street, Oxford OX2 6DP

Oxford University Press is a department of the University
of Oxford. It furthers the University's objective of excellence
in research, scholarship, and education by publishing worldwide.
Oxford is a registered trade mark of Oxford University Press in
the UK and in certain other countries

Database right Oxford University Press (maker)

Winnie and Wilbur: Winnie the Witch first published as Winnie the Witch in 1987
Winnie and Wilbur: The Midnight Dragon first published as The Midnight Dragon in 2006
Winnie and Wilbur: The Haunted House first published as The Haunted House in 2015
Winnie and Wilbur: Tricks and Treats first published in 2018

The stories are complete and unabridged

British Library Cataloguing in Publication Data available

ISBN: 978-0-19-276858-2

10 9 8 7 6 5 4 3 2 1

Printed in China

Paper used in the production of this book is a natural, recyclable
product made from wood grown in sustainable forests. The
manufacturing process conforms to the environmental
regulations of the country of origin

www.winnieandwilbur.com